SIGNORINA'S
DRAGON

MELINDA R. CORDELL

SIGNORINA'S DRAGON

PREQUEL TO THE
DRAGONRIDERS OF FIORENZA SERIES

Melinda R. Cordell

Rosefiend Publishing.

SIGNORINA'S DRAGON
Copyright © 2022 by Melinda R. Cordell

Ordering information: For details, contact the publisher at
hello@melindacordell.com
Cover design by Deranged Doctor Design
Book Formatting template by Derek Murphy @Creativindie

ISBN: 978-1-953196-59-0

The first chapter in this book is also the first chapter of Assassin's
Blade by the same author. Sorry about that! The rest of the story
is different after that!

First Edition: 8 June 2020

10 9 8 7 6 5 4 3 2 1 blast off!

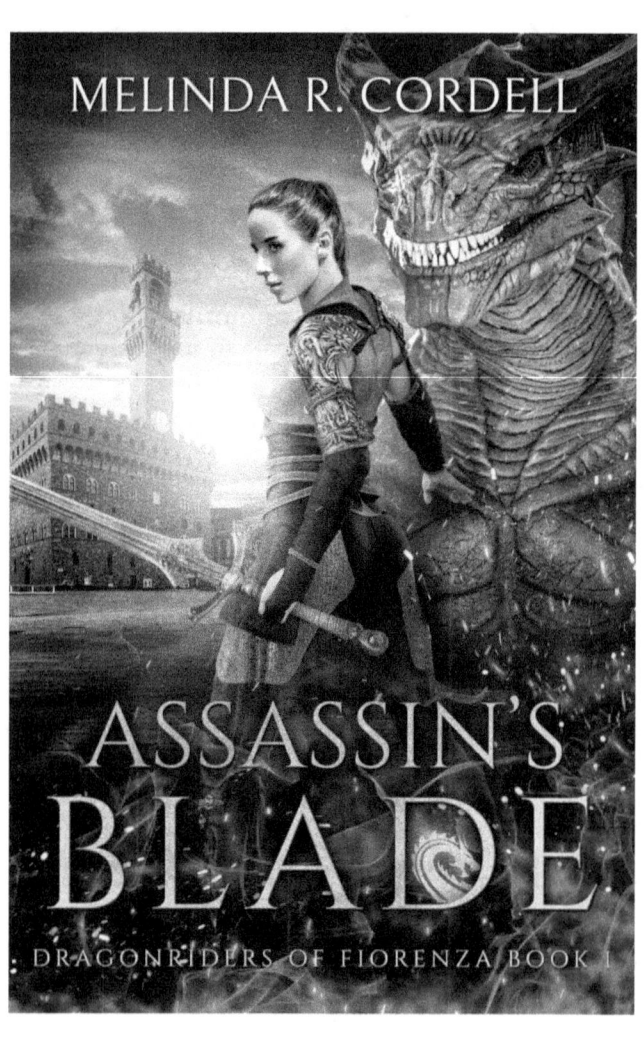

MELINDA R. CORDELL

ASSASSIN'S
BLADE

DRAGONRIDERS OF FIORENZA BOOK I

Book 1 – Assassin's Blade

**Wherein Fia and Neva are all grown up – but
now they're enemies.**

DRAGONRIDERS OF FIORENZA
SERIES ORDER:

Contents

THE END OF THE WORLD

Fia's target was in sight. She crouched behind a potted lemon tree in the piazza, a slip of a girl in an olive-green tunic and hose and boots, clutching her bow. Fia crooked her fingers at Neva to summon her over, her dark eyes never leaving the target.

Neva joined her, her blonde hair long and swinging loose around her face. Fia's dark brown hair was bound up, though not in the style of a married woman. Never that.

Neva rested her chin on Fia's shoulder, looking toward the target. "You better not do it," she whispered. "If you shoot him, the retaliation will never end. He will send his sultans and guards after you. They'll pursue you beyond the sunset to the gates of hell."

Fia plucked an arrow from her quiver. "I can outrun them. They can't kill what they can't catch."

Her target sat with his friends playing dice, a Persian form of the game from the old country, speaking in Syriac to his fellow countrymen and several Fiorenza friends.

The piazza was bustling with many people under the bright morning sun: some shopping, some visiting on their way to the well. The markets ran along the side of the monastery gardens, where breads, fruits and vegetables, and cheese were being sold, and the fragrance of bread and lemons and wood smoke hung over the piazza. Fia's target was sharing bread with his friends, still warm from the communal stone oven that had cooked it. He tore off a piece and lifted it in his fingers as he talked to his friends. There it stayed, aloft, as he continued talking.

Perfect. Fia drew the bow, her face pressed against the string as she took deadly aim.

"Fia, don't!" Neva whispered.

The bowstring sang, and the arrow flew to its mark – straight through the piece of bread, carrying it away.

"Aiee!" Her grandfather dropped what was left of his bread and he squinted at Fia.

Then he roared with laughter. "Child! That was my breakfast!"

The people he'd been speaking with were not amused. "Are you trying to put somebody's eye out?" one of his astonished friends said.

"Or get somebody killed?" another added.

Fia stood up from behind the lemon tree. "They're blunted arrows." Fia pulled out an arrow to show them. A little piece of leather was tied to the business end of the arrow. "And my aim is good. I wasn't going to hit any of you."

"Little girls shouldn't play with bows and arrows," one of the Fiorenza men said sanctimoniously.

"Little?" Fia said scornfully, hands on hips. "We're thirteen years old. We're not little."

"And *little* girls shouldn't wear their hair in that heathen style, and they shouldn't be talking back to their elders," the man added.

Grandfather tore off another piece of bread. "I am what you would call a heathen," he said mildly through his pepper-and-salt beard. "And in my home country, we allow women to shoot bows and arrows, and hold public office, and write books, and choose who they want to marry. If Fia were my grandson, you would be praising his aim and saying, 'Boys will be boys!'"

Grandfather's friend grumbled, eyeing Fia darkly. "All the same, this city-state is under the sway of the Pope. The holy Church in her wisdom says no to all those things."

"Your faith is cousin to my faith," Grandfather said. "I prefer my faith, for we treat our women as citizens, not chattel."

"And the girls can be assassins," Fia said to Neva, just loud enough for the other man to hear.

"I still think you shouldn't have shot that arrow," Neva whispered.

Fia bumped lightly against her side the way she did when she was bored at Mass. "Come on. Let's go play the Elder of the Mountain and his Many Assassins. We can be just like my grandmother, my teita Anna. I promise I won't make you shoot anybody."

"I want to be the old man of the mountain." Neva pulled her blonde hair into two sections, then brought them around to the front of her face and held them under her chin. "See? Now I have a white beard. Whitish."

"The Elder of the Mountain should have had a dragon army," Fia said.

"You're just saying that because you want to be a dragonrider," Neva said. She fluttered her beard at Fia, still holding her hair in front of her face. "We're assassins. We don't *need* dragons. You can't sneak around stabbing people with a dragon that's fifty cubits tall standing right behind you."

Fia rolled her eyes. "I don't care. I'm going to have a dragon. She will be a stealth dragon."

"Oh, so a fifty-cubit dragon is going to sneak around on its tiptoes?"

BOOM.

The great, hollow concussion reverberated in the air, a sound that Fia had never heard before. Her breath caught in her throat and she stopped in her tracks.

Neva dropped her hair. "What was that?"

All around the marketplace, talk died away. People raised their heads, looking around them. Even the sparrows in the lemon trees stopped their chirps.

Now a single-throated roar as of a thousand voices rang out from the direction of the boom.

Fia stood frozen on her feet. Inside the walls of the market, she could not see what was happening in the distance. Neva clutched her wooden sword. Fia took her best friend's hand as if to protect her.

"Fia, Neva," her grandfather called, leaning on the table for support as he got to his feet. "Both of you, go home. Now."

"What's happening?" Fia asked.

"We're in danger. Go."

BOOM. A second one, echoing through the houses and walls of the city. Another many-voiced shout.

"It's the city gate!" somebody shouted from the top of the market wall. "They're breaching the gate at the Via Paloma. To arms! To arms!"

"Who is breaching the gate?" Fia cried, but her voice was drowned in the chaos that broke out. Women screamed for their children. Shopkeepers started to their feet, drawing swords, some throwing their wares quickly back onto their mule carts. Heavy wooden shutters slammed shut over windows.

Suddenly, at Fia's back stood Teita Anna, her grandmother, so swiftly that Fia jumped. Teita Anna was barely taller than Fia, wearing her sand-colored scarf over her black hair. But her grandmother's presence made Fia suddenly feel safe, despite the panic rising around her, despite another BOOM that shuddered the air, followed by screams.

Teita touched a sash that she always wore as she watched the piazza intently. Fia knew that her knives were under that sash. Even all these years later, Teita kept several knives on her person, even though she hadn't worked as an assassin for years.

"What's happening?" Neva said nervously.

"The Sienese army is at the gates," Teita said. "You must go home at once."

"The Sienese army?" Neva gasped, her eyes lighting.

Fia quickly nocked a blunted arrow on her bow as the panic grew around them. If the Sienese army was here – another BOOM at the city gates chilled her blood – then that meant…

"That means the exiles have returned," Fia whispered. A large group of former citizens that had been exiled from the city had taken refuge in Siena, and the city had stood alone against Fiorenza for years.

And now they had arrived, all together, to bring war to Fiorenza.

"Yes," said Teita. "The exiles are trying to force their way back into the city."

Neva clutched her hands together. "My grandfather is with them." Enough people knew Neva's family – some barely tolerated them, knowing their connection with the exiles – that Fia was sure Neva would be in danger.

Teita clutched Neva's hand. "Don't show your joy," she said urgently, gazing into Neva's eyes. "If you want to get home safely, look afraid. Pretend to be frightened. Do you understand?"

"Yes, madam," Neva said, lowering her eyes. "But my grandpapa is probably in that army. He's come back." And Neva's eyes lit again with such hope that Fia nudged her urgently until she looked serious again.

Grandfather came hobbling up. "My leg will not let me run," he said. "Hurry home. I'll catch up."

Teita's eyes gentled with worry. "Take my dagger." She pulled her jeweled dagger. Even now, Fia marveled at the gleam of the ruby in its hilt, the keenness of its delicate silver blade.

Grandfather shook his head, very serious. "Keep it. Use it if necessary. I want the children safe at home. God go with you."

Just then a mother next to them screamed.

"Jacopo!" She gathered her other two toddling babies to her. The bundles she was trying to carry fell to the ground, but she didn't notice – her face was a mask of terror as she looked wildly around. "He's wandered away! Jacopo! Somebody find my baby!"

Teita went concerned. "I'll find him," she said, vanishing like the breeze.

Fia seized Neva's hand. "Let's run," she said. "Grandfather, can you keep—"

"A Sienese bitch!"

The shout cut through the chaos of the market.

Fia turned with a great gasp.

A man with a sword came running toward them. "Whelp! You will die for the sins of the exiles!" The man lunged, sword raised, toward Neva, who stood wide-eyed and afraid, trembling to the ends of her blonde hair.

It happened too fast for Fia to understand what she was seeing –

Her grandfather leapt suddenly between the attacker's sword and Neva, arms open.

The man came on too fast. The sword pierced Grandfather's chest.

Blood. So much blood.

Her grandfather crumpled to the stones of the piazza, choking out his life, a sword through his belly – but he was holding onto the sword's hilt as the attacker tried to pull it out, his dark, baleful eyes fixed on the man who would have killed Neva.

A cry wobbled from Fia's lips.

The next instant, a shriek like that of a bird of prey.

It was Teita, screaming with a sound that Fia would never forget.

Teita came flying across the marketplace like a hawk in its swift flight. A flash of silver and ruby as her jeweled dagger went flying – and a gout of blood flew from the man who had killed her grandfather.

The man flung his arms out, eyes wide, and slammed into the stones of the piazza.

Harsh shouts. Two more men ran across the plaza at Neva, swords drawn, murder in their eyes. "You killed Lapo!" they screamed.

Now Teita stood before both her dying husband and Neva. She reached under her sash, too quickly to see, pulled out something that glittered, and then swung her hand down hard. The first man cartwheeled in mid-run like a rabbit that had been shot. He crashed to the stones of the piazza, twitching, a knife sticking out of his neck.

The second man was nearly upon Teita. He spat at Teita and thrust his sword. Ducking his blade, she lunged into the man, using his running momentum to stab him deeply through the ribs. The next moment she shoved him back, stepping away as she pulled out her jeweled knife. The man's body fell, and a great gout of blood leapt from his wound with every beat of his heart. He lay sprawled on the pavement, the fountain of blood from his heart growing less and less.

Teita didn't have a drop of blood on her.

Her face crumpled with grief as she fell to her knees beside Fia's grandpa, her husband. Their eyes met.

Blood trickled from Grandfather's mouth as he whispered, "You are my wild bird, the love of my life."

"You have always held my heart within yours," Teita whispered, her tears flowing as she caressed his face.

"God give you peace," Grandfather said. Then a sigh flowed from his lips as if all the air went out of his lungs. His face went slack and his eyes drifted away from hers. He slipped from her arms and crumpled on the stones.

Fia pressed her fist to her mouth and screamed. She and Neva clutched each other.

Teita pulled the sword free from her husband's body, and with a moan of terrible grief she flung it aside. She turned her stricken eyes to Fia. "Go home now!" she screamed. "Protect your friend and take her home now! He gave his life to save hers!"

Fia was crying too hard to see, but Teita's voice galvanized her. The girls fled together, and Fia heard Neva's sobs through her own. Neva stumbled, half-fainting, and Fia threw her arm around her waist. "Keep going. Keep going," Fia sobbed, with no thought but the image of her grandfather crumpled over that sword. *He was holding on to the hilt,* she thought, *so the man couldn't pull it out and stab Neva ...*

"The tower," Fia gasped. "We'll go to my house ... we'll hide in the tower ..."

Neva and her family lived across the courtyard from Fia's house, the courtyard where children play, where a few storefronts opened into the street to sell meat and produce and a blacksmith kept his forge. All their lives, she and Neva had played tag or prisoner's base or dueling knights with the other children there.

Neva and Fia ran into her house and up the staircase that spiraled into the darkness, lit only by the narrow windows that had served as arrow windows in older times.

Moments later Fia and Neva stood upon the great tower of her parents' home. Awash in misery, Fia crouched upon the stones, her head in her hands. She couldn't stop sobbing. Neva sat next to her and gathered her in.

"Mother hen," Fia sobbed.

Usually Neva would cluck like a hen when Fia called her this. This time she just held her friend tighter, and Fia felt her tears upon her scalp.

"Your grandfather saved my life." Neva was shaking.

"I know."

"He was always so good to me," Neva said. "Those conversations we had when he was sitting outside at the end of the day … it was like he was my grandfather too."

"I know." Fia had always loved those easy conversations between the three of them as the sun went down.

Just then, a hissing in the sky.

"Look," Neva said, pointing, her voice wobbling.

Fia looked up. Over the parapets, Fia could see the dragons of the armies in the skies – more dragons aloft than she'd ever seen before.

The dragons of the Fiorenza army were rising into the air, their wings and scales flashing like jewels in the morning sun, and waves of billowing fire rolled out from them as they flew to meet the Sienese attackers in the air. The dragons that defended Fiorenza had asbestos banners with the picture of the lily upon them tied to their lower necks so the fighters and the armies on the ground could identify which side the dragons fought upon.

Their riders on dragonback shot at each other with crossbows as dragons lunged through the air. And through this came another BOOM from the gates.

Neva clutched Fia's hand in a grip that hurt, her face going pale. "My grandpa," she whispered. "He's in the Sienese army. He's come back."

Fia thought, *My grandfather will never come back.* But she wouldn't grudge Neva her excitement and hope. Neva had missed her own grandfather since he was driven from Fiorenza into exile when she was a little girl.

Fia looked into the skies as a phalanx of dragons from the Fiorenza army went roaring directly overhead: topaz and garnet war dragons, their wingspans wider than the roof of the tower that she and Neva cowered on. Sparks blew back from their breaths, and the sun made their scales gleam as if each were a brilliantly cut gem. The sun shone through the dragons' wings like the stained-glass windows at a cathedral, and the heat from their bodies as they passed overhead hit her like a blow. She'd always loved dragons and wanted desperately to be a dragonrider – but only men were allowed to fly dragons.

"Grandpa's come back," Neva whispered again, peeking over the parapet to look out toward the armies.

"His army might not succeed," Fia said. "The last time they tried this was…"

"No!" Neva said fiercely. "The Sienese army has got to succeed. They have to."

"But my family will be forced from the city if they do," Fia said, suddenly going pale, for her father was one of the twelve priors of the city – and he had signed the decree that had cast the rebels out.

"My family will have to leave if the army fails!" Neva said, as if suddenly realizing the same thing.

The Fiorenza dragons came flying to meet the Sienese dragons – and, as one, the Fiorenza dragons went abloom with fire.

The sky was aflame.

Even at this distance, Fia felt the heat from the skyful of dragons breathing fire, as if a second sun glared down from above. She had to turn her eyes from the white-hot blaze.

An emerald dragon fell out of the flames, bleeding badly from deep claw marks carved deep into its face – and the dragonrider on its back was all in flames, screaming such heart-rending wails that Fia immediately plugged her ears. The emerald dragon plummeted helplessly from the sky and crashed somewhere in the city. The stones vibrated under Fia's knees, and screams arose from where it had fallen.

The heat in the sky slowly abated.

Fia dared to look up then. More Sienese dragons were falling from the sky, or fleeing the oncoming wrath of the Fiorenza army.

Neva covered her mouth. "Oh, no, no, no …."

A great cheer went up from within the city walls. If the Sienese dragons had been pushed back, then the Sienese army at the gates had no protection from the Fiorenza dragons.

Screams from the Sienese army outside the gates as the conquering dragons of Fiorenza flew down for the kill.

Neva sobbed and put her face in her hands.

Fia put her arms around Neva. "Maybe he's not even in the attacking force," she said, hoping against hope this was true. "Maybe your grandfather was sick and couldn't fight …"

Just then, a familiar black horse came galloping through the narrow streets.

"Babbi!" Fia cried, leaning over the parapets. "Papa!"

Ahead of him came Neva's father on his own horse. "Get the wagon!" he ordered frantically as he came riding up to his house. "Get the wagon!"

Through her tears, Neva's eyes went wide. "The wagon? They're not going to make us leave, are they?"

"We can hide you," Fia said frantically, throwing her arms around Neva. If the Sienese army was being slaughtered outside their gates, the authorities would be doubling down on exiling any relatives who still lived within the walls – including Neva's family. "They can't make you leave. They *can't*. We can hide you … we make you out to be my new sister …"

"Where's Neva?" Babbi shouted below them, in the street.

"I have to go," Neva said, her eyes filling with new tears.

"No! Just hide." Fia clutched Neva's arm, frantic at the idea that she was going to lose her closest friend. And what would happen to a newly exiled girl and her family out there in the cruel world? Bandits and murderers lurked everywhere outside the safety of the city walls.

Except at that moment, Babbi burst through the door at the top of the tower, a great, black-haired, imposing man in his robes of state, his face blanched with rage.

Fia drew close to Neva, but he strode straight to Neva, grabbed her arm, and roughly dragged her down the stairs.

Neva cried out. "Please let go of me! I can leave! Ow!"

"Daddy, Babbi, what are you doing?" Fia cried, running after them down the dark stairs. Neva was sobbing, a sound that wrung her heart. "Let her go! What's the matter with you?" He'd never acted like this before, *never*.

"Get out, get out, get out!" he said as he dragged Neva outside and flung her into the street.

Neva's father ran over to him, threatening Babbi. "What the fuck is wrong with you?"

"Your daughter is a Lamb! I don't tolerate traitors in my home!"

"Babbi, she's not—"

"We are locking up the house," Babbi shouted at Fia. "Get inside, Fia, now!"

Fia grabbed Neva in an embrace. It was all happening too fast, and Neva's tears wrung her heart.

"This isn't fair – this isn't supposed to happen—" Fia said into Neva's shoulder as the girls clung to each other.

"I love you, Fia," Neva sobbed.

"I love you too, Neva. I hope your grandfather's safe, Neva, I—"

Something slammed into Fia's shoulder, and she yelped with pain. A rock!

"Get out of our city, you stinking Lambs," somebody shrieked. "Join the rest of the exiles, you sons of pigs!"

A stabler for Neva's family came galloping up with a horse and cart, and their servants and family began piling their goods into it. People gathered around their courtyard, screaming and catcalling at Neva's mother and sisters, hurling rocks at her father and laughing.

Babbi grabbed Fia and pulled her away from Neva.

"No!" Fia screamed, reaching back to Neva. "They're throwing rocks at her!"

"I said to get into the house, now!" He picked Fia up and carried her inside. "Bar the door!" he shouted at the servants, who were already slamming the thick oak shutters all over the fortress, and the rooms darkened with every slam. Mami was busily lighting the oil lamps and sconces.

Fia ran back to the door, fighting to lift the gigantic oaken bar, but Babbi scooped her up. "No. You will stay here."

"No! We need to help them. Help them, Babbi!"

"We cannot," Babbi said. He was trembling, his black curly hair quivering against his forehead. "Fia, if I lift one finger to help them, this city will have you and the rest of this family on a cart, leaving with the rest of the exiles, and they'll have me burned at the stake."

Fia struggled and kicked. "It's not fair! It's Neva! She's my best friend!" If she could just get away from him, she could save them herself. She was going to shield Neva with her own body if she could. Anything to let her friend know that somebody, *somebody* in this stupid city still loved her.

Babbi's arms were locked around her, and all her kicking and struggling didn't move them. Fia's hair clung to her sweaty face. So she bit his arm.

He dropped her, but before she could run he slapped her hard. She instantly burst into tears.

"You are *not* going out there." His voice was hard as iron. "Not on your life. Do you want those crowds to come for us? Do you want them to throw rocks at your brother and sisters? Do you want them to declare that we support the exiles, and drive us from the city as well?"

Fia was crying so hard that she couldn't speak.

Her father forced her to go upstairs. Once the family and servants were on the upper story, once he'd barred the door, she wrenched herself free and ran from him to the shuttered window overlooking the street, where she peered through a crack in the wood.

The last sight that Fia saw was of Neva running after her family and being pulled up into the overloaded wagon. She was clutching her favorite doll. Its wool stuffing was coming out of one leg where some brave grownup had ripped it.

She would never forget Neva's frightened eyes shining with tears from under her curly blonde hair as the wagon rolled out of the city, as long as she lived.

THE LONELY MOUSE

The smell of fires still lingered in the air, making Fia wrinkle her nose when she awoke the next morning. Her head still hurt from crying so much yesterday, and her eyes ached. She slowly sat up.

Grandpapa was dead. And her closest friend and her family had been driven out of the city. Forever.

Each thought hit her in its own wave of grief. She rolled over and buried her face in her pillow so she wouldn't be facing her little sister Bice, who was only five years old. Bice's own open-hearted sympathy had only made Fia cry more yesterday.

But from outside came the sound of chanting and shouting. Stupid people. "I don't want to look," she muttered. She curled up in bed, accidentally pulling the covers off of Bice, who made a sleepy protesting noise.

But then the voices got louder, and there was a crack. Crack. Crack. A final loud CRACK and a splintering noise. Then new shouting.

With a groan, Fia looked out the window to see what was happening … and cried aloud.

The cracking and splintering noises were from an excited crowd of people who had just broken down the door to the house where Neva used to live. Now they flung aside the battering ram and, stepping over the splintered remains of what remained of the oaken front door, laughed and shouted to their friends as they walked into Neva's family's house.

Seething, Fia threw on a dress over her shift, pulled on her boots, and ran downstairs quietly, trying not to wake her mother and father. If Papa knew she was sneaking out …

"He's not going to catch me," she muttered.

She unbarred the front door and ran out to where the crowd was now pushing their way in through the front door of her friend's house. The sound of crockery being smashed made her push forward through the crowd.

"No! Stop it!" Her voice was swallowed by the tumult of the people.

Somebody grabbed Fia's shoulder and pulled her back.

"Let me go!" she said, turning – but it was her grandmama, her teita, her eyes red with weeping.

Teita pulled Fia close to her body, and Fia smelled rosewater. "You must not go in," Teita said in a whisper. "These people have come to destroy the house."

Fia was so shocked that she couldn't speak for a moment. "But … but why!"

Teita frowned, watching the rabid crowd push in. "These backward people of this vindictive city-state have let their petty loyalties whip them into a froth. They scored a small victory yesterday, but now that they've cast out these citizens, they are tearing down their houses. They do this to make sure they can never return."

The words shook Fia to her very heart. She turned back and stared at the maddened crowd that was pushing its way into Neva's house. And now a new cruelty, for now Neva's family's clothes came floating down from the upstairs windows. People on the street pounced on them and tore them to rags, shouting, "Thus to traitors! Thus to the people who turned their backs on our fair city!"

Fia dashed toward the front door. Teita shouted behind her, but for the first time in her life, Fia managed to dodge her grasp.

If she hadn't been weeping so much for Giddo, my grandpapa, she would have caught me ... the thought came down like a weight on Fia's heart, but she pushed it aside as she shoved through all the idiots that crowded in Neva's front door. Some smug man blocked the door with his bulk, saying in a very self-satisfied voice, "The family who lived here can burn in hell."

Fia elbowed him in the junk as she pushed through. The man wheezed as if he'd been stepped on and then he doubled over.

"Sorry," she shouted in a very unsorry voice as she dashed through the house.

Upstairs, in Neva's family's bedroom, several people were milling around, throwing aside clothes and opening trunks, while an old lady from down the street was pulling handfuls of chicken feathers out of the mattress and stuffing them into a bag.

"Aye, there's little Portinari," sneered Monna Gatti, a neighbor, cutting her eyes at

Fia. "Are you sad that your little friend is gone? Your little traitor friend?"

Fia stared at her in open-mouthed shock for a moment before she could recover. "Your son is the same age as we are. We're thirteen years old!"

The older woman tsked at Monna Gatti as she paused in her mattress un-stuffing. "Leave the child alone. Signorina," the woman added, turning to Fia, "you may choose a memento of your friend, but then you must leave at once. This crowd will become violent. For the sake of your family, you must not be seen here again."

It was hard to hear this. Fortunately, just then Teita appeared in the bedroom doorway. "You heard her, Fia. Quickly."

Monna Gatti hissed and drew the sign of the cross at Teita, who took no notice.

Frantically, Fia looked around the room. There was Neva's trunk which had been opened and rummaged through. Neva's dolls were gone, the ones they'd played with all those winters ago. But on the floor, kicked next to the wall, was a familiar thing: The little stuffed mouse that was Neva's favorite toy when she and Fia were both little girls. She grabbed it up quickly.

"Did you find some trash that your little friend left behind?" Monna Gatti sneered. "Some trash to remember your trash friend?"

Fia clutched her little mouse friend to her chest, against her heart. *Her name is Squeaky,* was all that came to her mind, and tears rose to her eyes. She'd never really understood how cruel people could be.

Teita clutched Fia's arm. "Come," she said. "We must go, now."

They went down the stairs in silence though Fia trembled in every limb. Teita never let go of her arm.

Once they were out, Teita walked her away instead of walking across the street to their house. "We will go in through the scullery entrance, where those horrible people will not see us," she whispered. "And then you will not go outside for the rest of the day, whatever happens, whatever you hear. Do you understand?"

"No, I don't understand," Fia whispered back. "Why are they doing this? What's wrong with them? I hate them, I do!"

"Shh," Teita said, laying her fingers on Fia's mouth. "Not another word, or they'll come for our family, too. Not another word."

Fia, furious, half-wished they would. At least then her papa would understand how heavy her friend's burden was. At least then Fia could be with Neva. She could help keep Neva safe …

Once they were inside, Teita laid a heavy bar across the door, thumped it twice to secure it, then walked away to her quarters without another word.

Fia stood there, stupidly, listening to the muffled thumps and shouts outside until she was completely sick to her stomach. Finally she went to the bedroom where her mother and brother and sister were all looking out the window at the commotion in the street.

Fia slumped down to sit on the floor in the corner, gently stroking Neva's mouse. All she wanted, with all her heart, was to go see Neva. That was all she wanted.

The sounds from outside grew louder and louder – shouts at first and the sound of smashing wood. Then, later, came the thumps and crunch of falling stones and bricks, the clank of iron against masonry, the grunts of men, and loud crashes.

Later that morning, Fia looked out the window and saw, to her considerable astonishment, that the whole roof to Neva's house had utterly vanished, and a hole gaped in its side. The window through which she and Neva used to talk to each other had been completely demolished. Inside Neva's family's bedroom, where her friend used to sleep, all the beds and trunks had been smashed or thrown out. Now a group of cheering, sweat-drenched men swung pickaxes and hammers against the walls.

One of them, seeing Fia's indignant face staring at him, laughed. "Hello, little girl! We're tearing down the house of your traitor neighbors. Pretty soon you won't even have to look at this place any more. Won't that be nice?"

A gigantic chunk of stone in the wall suddenly teetered. "Look out below!" shouted one of the men, shoving it with one foot. Several others shouted, and one of them reared back and struck it hard with his sledge. The large piece of stone tumbled out of the wall and exploded on the street below with a huge bang. Cheers and whoops arose from the spectators.

Fia spun away from the window to throw herself across the bed with her hands over her ears.

She wished they would all die.

ADAMANTINE CHAINS

Fia finally managed to fall asleep. She was dreaming that her chickens had turned into mice and had gotten lost, when she was shaken awake.

"Fia," said her papa's voice, but he sounded excited for some reason. It was early afternoon, and the same noise of destruction continued from outside.

"Ugh. Stop." Fia pulled her blanket around her and rolled back over, trying to go back to sleep.

"It's no good for you to stay here in bed like this," Papa said, patting her on the shoulder. She pulled away from his touch. "Come. Wake up, Fia. I want you to go to the farm with me. I have something to show you."

From outside came a great shout, and then a huge crash and tinkle as if a ton of stone had fallen from some high tower. More cheering and laughter.

"I thought you wanted to stay here and watch your enemy's house be destroyed," Fia sneered into her pillow.

"Fia. Such talk. Now, you don't want to turn down this surprise that I have with you. Come." Her papa gave her his hand. "Shake off your sleep and come with me to the stables."

As angry as she was with Papa, she didn't want to stay here and listen to Neva's house be destroyed. Also, despite her anger, she couldn't help but be curious and puzzled. What kind of surprise required her to go all that way to the farm, a ride that took about two hours?

"Fine," she said groggily, picking up Neva's stuffed mouse. "I'll go."

Soon Fia and her papa were riding through the city. They passed through the first gate, then the second, and they were out of the city, riding into a hilly land of vineyards and trees. The air smelled of green and soil and blossoms. She breathed deeply of the fresh air, so welcome after the stink of woodsmoke and piss in the city.

They rode with a small, armed troupe who busily kept an eye out for highwaymen and bandits. She rode at her papa's side, talking, but burning with curiosity the closer and closer they got.

Soon, the fields of the family farm appeared, and the fortress that stood guard over it, a place where the farmers and workers who lived outside their walls ran to when villains came roving.

They soon reached the walls, where her father's soldiers waved to their compadres, and all were admitted through the eastern gate. Fia rode in behind her father …

… and as soon as she was through, her horse whickered and started dancing, despite all of Fia's best efforts to soothe her.

"Hold, hold," she said, trying to calm her palfrey. The other horses were also behaving badly, with their ears pasted against their skulls, snorting, and sidling back.

Fia leaned across her horse's neck. "Babbi, what is here?" Now she smelled something strange in the air inside the enclosed walls, something that smelled acidic and burnt. Worry twisted her stomach. She patted her pocket to make sure Neva's mouse was still safe.

Her father dismounted and gave his horse over to the stabler, who came hurrying up. "Let him take your animals. I'll wager they won't want to go farther."

Curious, Fia handed her reins over and followed her father around the corner to the courtyard … and as soon as she came around the corner, she stopped suddenly, her heart in her throat.

"A *dragon?*" Fia cried.

Papa gripped her arm, and she heard his sharp intake of breath. "Just *look* at that …" he sighed in wonder.

A real live emerald dragon sat in the center of the courtyard, hunched over itself like a wounded bird.

But then Fia saw the adamantine chains that bound the dragon. The chains looped its wings against its body so it was unable to open them. Its powerful front and back feet were manacled so it could barely walk.

"… But why?" Fia added under her breath, immediately angered by the sight of those chains on a dragon. How dare they!

The dragon's emerald scales had not been cleaned since the battle, blackened with soot and scorch. It was trying to groom an emerald wing with long licks of its tongue, dodging the chains wrapped around its middle that that bound its wings against its sides. It seemed to grimace, as if in pain.

Fia couldn't get over the size of this great being. If it had been able to open its wings – she wished that the dragon could open its wings – she was sure they would have been as big as sails.

Her heart was hammering. She'd never been this close to a dragon before. They looked lovely in the skies, like oversize birds. But up close, the creature was about as large as two horses, with heat rippling off it.

"Can you believe it?" her papa asked softly, his hands on her shoulders. "Look at it. A dragon in my courtyard!"

The dragon, seeming to notice them for the first time, looked up from its wings with a low, dangerous-sounding growl. It panted as its yellow, reptilian eyes fixed on Fia and her papa and didn't move. A light scrim of smoke floated up from its mouth.

Fia took two steps back, her mouth open.

The dragon's eyes were yellow with a black slit in the center, like the eyes of the tiny fire-lizards that sunned themselves on the stone walls of her house.

To have the dragon's eyes on her made Fia feel like a mouse under a hawk's eye. She felt herself shrink.

"Papa?" She leaned toward him, not daring to take her eyes off the dragon. "What if we make it mad? What if it blasts fire at us?"

Papa smiled. "He wouldn't do anything like that. They're strictly trained not to blast fire outside of battle."

This did nothing to assuage her fear.

Nevertheless, she said, "But Papa ... the chains. Why?"

"I'm afraid the chains have got to stay on for our safety until it can earn our trust. You hear people prattling on all day about how dragons are tamed. But, deep down, they really aren't – especially when they're wounded as badly as this one."

Fia nodded, unable to catch her breath, frightened and awestricken at the same time. This thing was enormous. Even from here she could feel the heat coming off the dragon's body. Its scales glowed like embers in an emerald fire, the fire's light moving through them as the breeze brightened its light.

The dragon now turned its head more toward her, gigantic as a shield and covered with horns. But this movement revealed a huge gash on its side, a gash so deep that Fia almost felt its wound on her own side.

"Papa! Look, it's hurt."

"I know, honey. I know. That's why it's here."

"What?"

But just then, before Papa could explain, Ser' Corso Valori came strolling up from the main house. "You've arrived!" he called, and at his loud voice, the dragon jumped slightly, rounding on him. Valori took no notice, walking swiftly to Papa. "Why, Folco, I see you've met the war dragon," he said. "What a beauty, no?"

Papa and Valori warmly took each others' hands and shook them, greeting each other. They'd been friends for all of Fia's life, and both served on the Council of Twelve that ran the affairs of their great city.

"I didn't expect to see such a marvelous specimen here, to be honest," Papa said, staring back at the dragon. "I can't remember when I've seen an emerald that's so large."

"She's a rare one, no doubt about it," Valori said. "She's a Sienese war dragon, but she's been wounded and needs to retire." He gestured at the dragon's wing, which had been torn badly. One of its front legs had a terrible gash that continued up its neck. Somebody had salved the wound, but the sight of the blood and open flesh made young Fia woozy.

Her father put an arm around Fia. "This is our dragon now," he said proudly.

Fia twisted around in Papa's embrace to look at him in amazement. "What? What did you just say?"

Papa lifted a hand toward the dragon. "She's ours now. How do you like that?"

SPAWN OF HELL

All Fia could manage in her amazement were some "blub blub" sounds. Her papa and Valori laughed.

"Ours?" Fia gasped, staring at the dragon with amazement. "This dragon?" It was as if Valori had flung open a treasure chest overflowing with gold, pearls, and rubies and said, *This belongs to you now, all of it*. She couldn't get her head around it.

Valori nodded, then became serious. "Her rider was killed in yesterday's battle," he said. "Burned to death. It was a bitter fight, though our side gained the victory and held the exiles off. But you can see the toll it's taken on this dragon," Valori said, stretching a hand out to it. Its eyes narrowed and it drew back. "She likely got those wounds while grappling with one of our dragons."

"How did you get a whole entire dragon?" Fia asked in awe. She couldn't even breathe, she was still so amazed. Her papa patted her on the shoulder, smiling.

"I captured it from the Sienese army," Valori said grandiloquently, puffing up like a frog, which amused Fia every time he did it.

Papa shot him a quizzical look, raising an eyebrow. "Captured it with your bare hands, did you?"

"Well, technically," Valori added, deflating slightly, "I didn't capture it all by myself. The dragon fell from the sky, badly wounded, its dragonrider dead on its back. It was so stunned that our dragons had no difficulty capturing it, though it attempted to put up a fight. Since it fell to earth so close to your fortress, it was no trouble to bring it here."

"So you didn't capture it all by yourself," Fia said.

"Well, no," Ser' Valori said meekly.

Papa laughed. "Well done! Now you don't have to confess the sin of pride to the priest."

Valori puffed up again. "Now you see, young lady, I am giving this dragon to your papa as a token of our esteem for him and his steadfast loyally to the city of Fiorenza. A man of his caliber should absolutely have his own dragon."

Papa turned pink and shook his head modestly. "You overestimate me."

"Nonsense!" Valori blustered. "Nonsense! You've worked valiantly for years with precious little recognition. But that's all changed, my friend, starting with yesterday's excellent rout."

They went on in this way, giving praise and deflecting the praise modestly, but just then Fia stopped hearing everything they were saying because the dragon fixed its yellow eye on Fia, and as far as she was concerned, everything else vanished.

Fia, feeling very small and scared, shrank down into herself under its eye, like a mouse that had looked up into the eye of a hungry hawk. She felt as if it judged her and found her wanting. Why would this grand, glorious animal have anything to do with her?

Their voices came filtering back into the moment she had with the dragon. "You did us a favor, Folco," Valori was saying. "You stood, steadfast, at our side, when the Sienese bastards and the exiles were pursued out of our glorious city."

Including Neva. At the thought, Fia was furious again.

"At any rate, this Sienese dragon, this beautiful war dragon, is yours now," Valori said grandly. "It can be your personal ferry animal. A fitting tribute to the impotence of their army."

"I don't know, Corso." Her papa shook his head as he looked at the great emerald beast, which now shifted his reptilian eyes to him. "Raising a dragon takes a lot of money and resources. I must confess that I am not sure I should take on this responsibility."

"Nonsense!" Valori cried again, thumping Fia's papa vigorously on the back until he choked. "You alone of all the council are dragonless. We cannot let such a shameful state of affairs continue. And it would be so much more relaxing for you to fly your own dragon to those endless meetings that you are always attending in other cities, instead of riding a horse. You must admit, it would be so much better to go on dragonback so you can be home in time for supper with your beloved family."

Papa's face softened as he looked at his daughter, then at the dragon. This very point had been something he'd complained about often, every time that he'd come home late, smelling of horse after a long ride from some distant city.

Valori continued. "We don't believe this animal will be able to recover from these wounds enough to fight in our army. So once this dragon heals, you can make it your ferry animal when you fly to Siena to wring the terms of peace from those traitors, those backstabbers. What a sight you will be! And then the greatest members of Siena's fallen army must watch you fly into their city, riding their best war dragon as if he is a broken-down old ferry animal. Let it drive home to them how impotent they truly are."

Papa gazed at the dragon, a new look coming into his eyes. "I like that," he said simply.

Valori turned to Fia. "And I also give this dragon to you, dear child, to make up for the death of your grandfather … and for the loss of your best friend."

Fia's eyes widened, and even as they filled with tears, she wondered if she'd heard him correctly.

"I, too, have lost dear friends to exile," Valori said gravely. "I, too, have watched my closest companion, one who was to me as Jonathan was to King David, be driven from our city like a common criminal. I never spoke to him again, though I have looked for him for years, in every city I traveled to. So I can understand how you have been doubly bereaved. Perhaps this beautiful creature can help ease your grief, insofar as this is possible."

Papa's arm went around Fia's shoulders and he gave her a gentle squeeze.

"You are very kind," she murmured as if she were a high-born old lady.

"Your family deserves nothing but the best," Valori said gallantly. "Now come! Let us see if it will be friends with you, so you may command it as is your right." He pulled out a crop and smacked it against his leg.

Fia's forehead furrowed. *Really?* At the snap of the crop, the dragon narrowed its eyes.

"When we captured this animal and muzzled it, it was rampaging and raging," Valori said. "Look at it now, cowering and subdued. The only way to tame a wayward dragon is to beat it with whips!"

Fia nearly began scolding Ser' Valori, but then she saw the dragon rise up from behind him like an emerald mountain.

Its scales started to glimmer, like embers when a strong wind blows over them. It rose, its eyes never leaving Valori, smoldering, and Fia saw the glint of teeth in its mouth.

She was sure the dragon had its own plans.

Fia backed away. "Ser, put away your crop. The dragon looks angry."

"Nonsense!" Ser' Valori said, snapping the crop again. "Look, it has been humbled and brought low after the defeat of its rider—"

The wounded dragon lunged, its jaws open.

Valori sprang back with his mouth open in sudden panic. The dragon's teeth snapped shut where Ser' Valori had been only an eyeblink before – missing him, literally, by the skin of the dragon's gleaming teeth.

The dragon's chains rang like angry cymbals, but it was too hobbled to spring forward, and it stumbled, then collapsed, chest first, against the ground. It struggled to rise, tail lashing, murder in its yellow eyes.

Valori released a stream of curses, drawing his sword. "You accursed dragon, you spawn of hell!" he shouted. Then he paused a moment in his curses to slap out the small fires that had been started on his clothes by the clash of the dragon's teeth and the sparks they'd flung out.

"Corso, please," Fia's papa said. "Good heavens."

"We subdued your sickening people when you tried to break through our gates yesterday!" Valori shouted at the dragon. "We subdued them and drove them to rout!"

The dragon merely reared back, teeth gleaming. Its scales flushed again and a flame winked at the back of its throat.

"Stop!" Fia cried, throwing out her hands. "Stop! What are you trying to do?"

At her cry, both dragon and Valori stopped, staring at her with amazement.

"Child, it is not your place to speak," her father said.

Confused, surprised by the result of her cry, the only thing she could think of to say to Valori was, "What are you trying to do, lose the rest of your hair in a fireball?"

And she inwardly cringed. She was just trying to keep Valori from being mad at her for scolding him.

But Valori turned, with a mock gasp. "I have plenty of hair!" he said, his hand flying to his receding hairline.

Relieved by his playing along with her joke, Fia was able to smile. "Then for the love of God, leave that dragon alone!"

He turned the mightiest of frowns upon her, drawing himself up as if he entertained great scorn for the world. Then he subsided with a chuckle. "Well, well, little girl. From the mouths of babe and suckling children, indeed."

"I'm thirteen years old," Fia said, now indignant for real. "I'm no baby. But at the same time, don't make the dragon upset, please. I'm too young to die!"

At that, Valori roared with laughter.

Fia gazed at the dragon which was staring coldly at the men with its bottom jaw jutting out maliciously. But it wasn't clacking its jaws or trying to attack now. Fia had managed to defuse the situation, and nobody was angry at her over it. She stood a little straighter.

"Now, this dragon needs someone to help rehabilitate her and bring her back to fighting trim," Valori told Fia, gazing at her gravely.

Fia's heart dropped. She shot a confused glance at Valori, then her father, then the dragon. "Um … who's going to do that?"

Papa shook his head at his friend. "Listen. I know of someone here in this village who is skilled in dragon work. He can handle that work."

Fia deflated at that, and Papa noticed. "No, chicklet," he said. "You're too young, and dragon work is too dangerous, as you just saw. No argument."

She wanted to be friends with that dragon, the best friends the world ever saw. And if she really made friends with the dragon ... then she could fly out to Neva and try and help her. She could bring her friend back and they could play again.

Just as if nothing had happened.

A Final Goodbye

Fia missed Neva. As they rode their horses back home, Fia imagined flying the dragon to find Neva. They'd be so happy to see each other again and the dragon would protect them both on their adventures in travelling the world.

That night when were nearly home, Neva's home came into view. Fia sucked in a breath as soon as she saw it. Neva's house was torn halfway down, a pile of rubble lying in the street in front of the ruined structure.

Papa glared hard at Fia. "Not a word out of you," he said, trying not to move his lips.

"But ...."

"No." Said in such a hard, angry voice that it shocked the tears out of her eyes.

Why are you afraid of what those assholes think? Why should you care what they think at all? She pressed her lips together to hold in all the angry words that she wanted to spew out.

It wasn't until they stabled the horses and went into the house that she pulled away from Papa and went back up to her own room. But she stopped before she went up the stairs.

"I don't want to stay here, in this house," she told Papa. "Not while they're tearing Neva's house down."

"But your grandfather's funeral is tomorrow."

Fia gritted her teeth and turned away, but she said no more because she was too close to tears to speak. Her poor grandpapa.

So the next day, her family left the house for his services. Fia tried not to look at the obscene crowd hooting and screaming as they tore apart her friend's house, stone by stone, and they made their way to the mosque for the procession, service, and burial.

Once the burial was finished, Teita dropped a glittering golden ring into her husband's grave and then went up into her room and shut herself in without a word. Her grandparents had always been so devoted to each other.

But now Fia's world had fallen apart. Her Teita, though distant, had always been with her to teach her how to fight like an assassin, how to move in secret through a crowd, and how to talk to kings and sultans and caliphs if you were on a secret mission.

But Grandpapa would bring home sweets for her and sneak them to her and Bice. He always went with them to explore the river and look at bird's nests in the trees. He'd sit with Neva and Fia in the evenings and talk to them about his childhood in Syria, his life in the old village, the roses that bloomed in his papa's garden, and the books that his mother used to read. A kind and gentle soul, his weathered hands would cradle a baby bird, or Fia and Neva's hands, or the honey drops he was always giving them.

"I want to help the dragon," Fia told papa as they returned home.

He gave her an odd look. "You aren't a healer."

"I'm more of a healer than you are," she said sternly.

"You're not old enough to live out there alone," Papa muttered.

"What do you mean, alone?" Fia asked. "My old nurse lives in the village there, not far from our farmhouse. I have cousins there and people who have known me since I was a little baby. I just lost my best friend and my grandpapa. In a way I lost my grandmama because of this," she burst out. "And then, all day long, I have to listen to these bastards tearing down my friend's house where we played for many happy hours. That is why I want to go back to the farm, and stay there, and take care of the dragon."

"You aren't going to take care of any dragon, I promise you," Papa said sternly.

"I don't care. Ser' Valori said that the dragon was for me, too. I want to work with it." *And make friends with it,* she didn't say.

"Pah! I want you to not be burned to death. You saw what it tried to do to Corso."

"Ugh! I'm not going to act like a jerk next to the dragon."

Now Papa stared at her. "How could you say such a thing bout Corso?"

"He should have been paying attention to the dragon. He shouldn't have been making fun of it."

"I don't care. I'm not going to let you near that dragon," Papa said.

Just then, Teita appeared, leaning heavily on the doorframe, her eyes red-rimmed, and her face puffy with weeping.

"Enough," she said, her voice gravelly. "No more of this. Folco," she said to Papa, "if you have any regard for me, you will fulfill the child's request. She will go to the farm. I'll take her myself if I have to."

Papa went pale but shook his head. "No," he said in a defeated voice. "No, I'll … I'll take her."

"Good," Teita said firmly. "Your daughter should not have to endure watching her friend's house torn down to the foundations – whatever *your* feelings happen to be about the situation."

Papa's face flushed now, and Fia was glad of it.

His eyes met hers. "I'll take you back," he said. "Maybe you should go out to the farm and stay there, just if only to get out of your mama's hair for a while."

He seemed ready to say something else, then simply shut his mouth and left the room.

Well, fine. It didn't matter why she went, just so long as she could go.

She turned to thank Teita, but her grandmother was already turning away and walking to her room to shut the door. Her sobbing began again as soon as the bolt clicked.

Fia sat at the window, looking out over the ruins of Neva's home. She wasn't going to stay here. She refused. Neva was gone, and Fia didn't have anybody to talk to. Bice was only five years old. Papa was too busy with official work to listen to her. Mama was always busy with the little kids, especially her baby brother who hadn't been named yet because he was so sickly.

She couldn't get her teita's sobbing out of her head. Her sobs made Fia feel so lost and alone, listening to them.

The next morning, Papa went with her to the farm, and they had little to say to each other. She didn't want to talk to her papa and her head was full of ways to bypass him so she could work with the dragon too.

A Few Cups of Wine

The first thing her papa did when they arrived at the farm was take Fia to her old nurse's house. Messer and Signora Albizzi lived in a tidy (and tiny) home that barely fit the two parents and their son, who was Fia's age.

"Fia can sleep at our farmhouse," Papa said, but Signora Albizzi, who Fia used to call Nursey but now called Rosana, said, "Tut tut, we don't mind your daughter's company at all. She may stay with us, if she likes."

Rosana, who was now too sickly to work, bustled inside and brought out an extra chair for Fia while Papa went out to tend to the dragon. "Now watch," Papa told Fia. "Watch how I bend this dragon to my will."

Rosana dragged a chair to Fia, and also brought a jug of wine and two old wooden cups that Fia used to drink out of when she was little. "Well," the old nurse said philosophically, pouring Fia a drink, "settle in, child. This should be interesting."

Papa spent the next couple of hours bending the dragon to his will by dodging its teeth and ducking its claws. Though he tried to make it allow him to ride, it would not let him approach him at all. Every time he tried, it snapped at him. Though the dragon was still chained and manacled, it was no longer muzzled as it had been when it was first captured, when it had been addled from its fall and unable to fight back.

After a little while, Papa further bent the dragon to his will by standing well out of its reach and swearing at it.

The whole time, Fia sat with Rosana in front of her house, watching the show while sipping wine and talking.

"So have you bent the dragon to your will yet?" Fia asked as Papa came back to them, hot and sweaty.

"Yes. There's a method to it." Papa picked up their wine jug, took a big drink straight from the bottle, and went back to bending a dragon to his will – which, at this point, consisted of him standing under a tree glaring balefully at it.

Fia and Rosana fell into conversation about the old days, and said hello to Messer Albizzi, who stopped by to give his wife a peck on the cheek and to drink a cup of wine before he and their son went back to work thatching roofs.

"What is your papa doing this time?" Messer Albizzi asked Fia in a low voice.

Fia looked up. Now her papa was trying to sneak up behind the dragon with a saddle, as if the dragon were some old horse he could trick.

"Don't you know? He is clearly bending the dragon to his will," Fia said.

Rosana's husband watched Fia's papa for a long moment.

"Hmm," was all he finally said.

Papa tried to throw the saddle over the dragon's back, but the dragon, not even bothering to stand up, grabbed the saddle in its teeth – her papa barely let go of the thing in time – and flung it away over the treetops.

Messer Albizzi groaned. "Oh, not *again*," he said, and trudged off to find it.

"Try tempting the beast with a haunch of goat," Rosana called to Fia's papa.

"Pat it on the nose," Fia added. "Dragons like it when you pat them on the nose."

Papa merely shot them an exasperated look just before the dragon's tail snaked in and knocked him off his feet. He landed with an *oof!* in the dust as the dragon looked on with satisfaction.

Rosana said, "Yes, your papa is most assuredly bending the dragon to his will," and poured a little more wine into Fia's wooden cup.

"I'm definitely learning a lot by watching this. As in, what not to do," Fia said as they drank.

That evening her papa, who was quite worn out after having bent the dragon to his will, climbed on his horse to travel back home, joining an armed band of travelers that was going by.

"I'm *allowing* you to stay here, understand," he told Fia as he leaned off the side of his horse.

"Oh, yes, certainly," she agreed.

"Messer Albizzi will take care of the dragon while I'm away. You can watch, but remember that a dragon responds best to strong discipline. And you are not allowed to work directly with the dragon. Leave that to the men who know best. Do you understand?"

"Well, I certainly have no intention of bending the dragon to *my* will."

"A wise choice," Papa said, and he rode away.

Fia watched them canter down the road, a cloud of dust rising from the horses' hooves, the murmur of conversation from the people, the jingle of halters, the slow thud of hooves. She watched until they vanished among the trees and only an occasional glitter from a spear came back to her.

"Good," Fia muttered, and went back to the house.

Her nurse was full of stories about the old days when Fia was a little girl and did things like eat bugs and collect snakes. They ate supper outside in front of the house with Rosana's husband and son. The son, Salvi, was an acne-ridden boy about Fia's age, so they studiously ignored each other, doing everything in their power not to make eye contact or even acknowledge each others' presence.

Then, once the sun had set, Rosana tucked Fia into her little bed exactly the same way she used to when Fia was little. She even sang the same song about the sleepy little duck, which Fia had forgotten about.

"I'm thirteen years old, you know," Fia protested with a yawn.

Her old nurse just tutted, "Yes, yes, a very mature thirteen," and blew out the candle.

A Gory Breakfast

Fia awoke very early the next morning. Outside in the predawn darkness, she heard Messer Albizzi singing outside. He worked for Fia's father as the stabler and factotum for the whole farm, so he was always up early to take care of the flocks and other livestock on the farm.

Fia quickly dressed and went outside, following the music. He was singing a song from some barbarian land in the north:

> *I never knew aught of terror*
> *Till today when the berserks came.*
> *They sailed to my isle in their ashen ships,*
> *All twelve devoid of shame,*
> *And landed with many a whoop and yell,*
> *Those wretches of evil fame.*

The music led her to the open patch of land with a great barn that was built back in the time of the Emperor Aurelius, back in the day of the old Romans. The dragon sat just inside the barn now, its manacled legs tucked uncomfortably under its body. It watched Messer Albizzi very intently with its reptilian gaze as the man shut the gate to the goat pen and turned around.

"Buongiorno, little mite," he said, noticing Fia by the light of the lantern.

He carried an old goat under his arm, pressed against his side to keep it from escaping. It jerked slightly, trying to pull away, but was otherwise being fairly obedient while its face and eyes were covered. The dragon, still manacled, was watching the goat intently.

Salvi was feeding the goats. He scowled when he saw Fia and kept his distance. He used to be a decent person – *To be fair,* Fia thought, *he probably still was* – but once his voice started changing, he spoke as little as possible to Fia and looked miserable all the time. However, she was just as awkward and uncomfortable around him – not that this made anything any better.

Up close, in the darkness of early dawn, the dragon loomed, gigantic and gleaming, in the darkness. Its front two feet were bigger than a man's head, and had thick claws about the size of Fia's hand. Its teeth gleamed by the lantern's light, set in a wide jaw – a jaw that could effortlessly bite her in half.

Its loyalties still lay, clearly, with its fallen rider. Fia was sure that the dragon had no intention of letting anybody else ride her.

Those chains, though … Fia's blood boiled every time she saw those chains on the dragon's legs and wings. They were adamantine chains, nearly impossible to break, even for a dragon that breathed flames. She desperately wanted to unlock them and set the dragon free, even if that meant seeing it fly away – forever.

Messer Albizzi set the lantern on the top of a nearby fence post. "I'm going to butcher this goat now. Do you need to look away?"

Fia did. She heard the bright ring of the knife as he pulled it from its sheath, and she cried a little at the goat's plaintive cry, until its cry faded out and died away. She always hated that part.

But when she turned back, the dragon was lifting its head off its taloned feet. Even in the dim light, Fia could see how blackened and scorched they were.

"See how badly the dragon needs cleaning?" Messer Albizzi said, deftly skinning the goat. "But she still won't let me near her ... though that may be about to change, I hope."

"Maybe," she said dubiously, as the dragon stared, its yellow eyes, lizard-like, unblinking, fixed only on the freshly-killed goat. It rose slightly, an impatient movement. "How can you get close enough to feed it? What if it blows fire on you?" Fia added.

"That shouldn't be anything to worry about," Messer Albizzi said after finishing his work, setting the hide aside for cleaning and tanning later. "These dragons have been trained against using their fire outside of war since they were hatched from eggs."

Now he picked up the freshly butchered goat and met the dragon's eye. "Come, my friend," he said soothingly to the dragon. "Come, now. I know you are hungry, yes? I will put this down so you can eat it. Don't bite me, for then there will be nobody to feed you, and then you'll be so sad, such a sad dragon. I know you don't want that, do you?"

Speaking softly, moving slowly, he advanced to within the dragon's reach. Messer Albizzi's eyes never left the dragon, and the dragon's eyes never left the goat. Slowly, he lay the goat down within reach of those enormous jaws. The dragon sat up at attention, shivering with the effort it took to sit still.

Then he stepped back quickly, saying "Eat, friend."

The dragon lunged out to the length of its chains and devoured the goat, swiftly choking it down in gory chunks. Fia was disgusted and fascinated at the same time.

"How long have you worked with dragons?" Fia asked, opening her eyes again once the sound of eating had abated.

"I was a dragon stabler when I worked with the Fiorenzian army." He watched the dragon trying to clean its manacled legs with little success. "I spent many long hours on the march with the dragon herds, keeping the livestock in good health and fighting off any raiders, whether from outside the army or within the ranks. I learned how to quickly separate animals from out of the herd and kill them. It's a little more complicated than what you'd expect, especially when we were on the march, but I had a good reputation for keeping everything in order and giving each dragon the right-sized animal so it would be full but not stuffed. You don't want to give a heavy eater a tiny goat. Like with this one," he added, for the dragon was now crunching the bones and staring hard at Messer Albizzi. "Did you see how quickly Signora Flame ate her goat? She's starving. I'm going to give her a second one. Salvi! Catch the red kid that's skipping over in that corner and bring her to me." Salvi stared blankly at his father for a moment, then went in through the gate, looking around.

"Why do you kill the goat before you give it to the dragon?" Fia asked, watching Salvi wrestling a goat out of the pen.

"It's more humane. You don't have to worry about the goat running away if the dragon's first bite doesn't kill it. You don't have to worry about a dying goat accidentally hooking the dragon in the eye with a shit-covered hind hoof. Furthermore, the dragon doesn't digest the hide very well, so I have them tanned so I can make boots and gloves for people in the village who need them."

Fia's eyebrows went up. "That's a lot."

"I was charged with taking care of living creatures. I intend to treat them with as much compassion as I want to be treated."

"Instead of beating them with whips to break them."

His face darkened slightly. "Yes," he said. "But you know better, don't you?"

Fia nodded vigorously.

"Good girl. A dragon has better things to do than to be bent to a man's will."

"Be Brave"

That morning after Mass and after breakfast, Fia returned to the old oak tree near the dragon. The dragon was snoozing, but when Fia walked under the tree, its eyes popped open and she jumped to her feet like a mountain suddenly uprooting itself. Its tail lashed once, then it went still, staring at her.

Fia had frozen as well, her breath stopped in her throat, at the deadly stillness of the dragon. Then she slowly walked to the tree and sat down at its base. It was uncomfortable, but she found a spot that was less uncomfortable and leaned back against the tree, just watching the dragon glittering in the sun.

The dragon didn't move for a long time. Then, slowly, it sank back down, so slowly that it was hard to notice it was moving while Fia was watching.

They just sat there, together, in each others' presence, and Fia didn't say a word.

She sat there until suppertime, not doing anything – just looking into the branches and watching the patterns the leaves made against the blue.

That evening, Messer Albizzi's son came out sullenly. The dragon once again sprang to its feet, but he ignored it. "Mama says you need to come eat," he said. Then, with a glance at the suspicious dragon, he left.

Fia sighed and, with a glance at the dragon, she said, "I'll see you later, okay?" The dragon didn't move. Its wings were pressed against the manacles that held them as if she wanted to throw them wide. Fia wished she could take the off, but knew it would fly away almost immediately the moment they were removed.

She had to sit next to Salvi at the table, which was awkward. Though he was joking with his father, he clammed up as soon as Fia walked in. The jerk. Even worse, he was left-handed and she was right-handed, and the minute they started eating, their elbows clashed.

Fia frowned and got more aggressive in defending her space. He did, too, jostling a bite of mutton off her fork and onto the floor, where one of the dogs immediately inhaled it.

"Stop that!" Fia said. Pretty soon they had their arms with their forks in them locked in mortal combat.

"You children need to stop or I'll give your food to the hogs!" his mother said. "Both of you! Fia, I thought you were better raised than that."

Her face flaming, she finished her dinner and retired back to the tree. As soon as she saw the dragon, it bounced to its feet once again, all suspicion.

This time she gathered grasses and leaves to make a softer seat, and sat down at last. The dragon stayed standing for a long time.

It was just beginning to sink down when Salvi came out of the house. Immediately the dragon was up on its feet again.

"What are you doing?" Fia snapped.

"Coming out to see why you're sitting under a tree like this all day."

"I'm trying to get the dragon used to me. Keep your voice down."

"He's still scared."

"It's a she, and of course she's scared. She had her rider killed and she was captured by the enemy – us."

"Don't matter," he said sullenly. "You have to break a dragon in the same way you break a horse."

"Not by beating it with a whip," she said.

"We don't beat them with whips," he said scornfully. "You act like we've never seen a dragon before, or worked with them. Have *you*?"

"Sure. Lots of times," Fia lied.

His eyes narrowed. "Did not."

"Did too."

He waved a hand at the little seat of grasses and leaves she'd just made. "So what's this?"

"A soft place for my butt."

"No, all this. Sitting under a tree all day looking at a dragon. How's this supposed to tame a dragon?"

"Were you watching me all day?" she snapped.

His face turned bright, bright red. "No! I have more important things to do!" Then he spun on his heel and left abruptly.

"So do I!" she yelled after him.

"Good!" he shouted over his shoulder.

"Fine!"

She watched him go. What an idiot! To be honest, she was trying to tame a dragon in the same way she'd once trained a cat, but she didn't want to tell him that. She'd tamed a wild cat that had been hurt in this same way. She'd closed the cat in a shed and sat next to it over the next few days until it had warmed up to her. She never forgot her thrill of joy when she felt its cold nose touch the back of her leg – just a small touch and the brush of its whiskers. He was still hesitant and shy around people but he eventually let her pet him.

Taming a dragon in this way sounded stupid, to be honest, now that she thought about it.

The next morning she went out with Messer Albizzi. She tried not to cover her eyes when he killed the goat, but failed. She should have been used to this by now, but she was tenderhearted, as Papa always said.

"Do you want to help me feed the dragon?" Messer Albizzi asked.

She looked at the limp goat and then at the dragon, who was standing up, but shivering very subtly while staring at the dead goat.

"I'll … try," she said. As much as she wanted to get close to the dragon, she was quickly changing her mind, now that she stood before it with nothing to protect her from the dragon's teeth and fire. A thread of smoke rose from its jaws, and she felt its heat radiating off it.

Be brave, Fia. Something that her grandpapa always said to her, ever since she was a little girl. *Be brave, little flower.*

She gingerly picked up the dead goat by the hooves … but then she saw Salvi watching her from over by the goat pen.

Resolve flooded her. She wasn't going to cower in front of him. She knew what she was doing!

"Dragon," she said soothingly, coming forward under its yellow eyes. Her heart was pounding, but the dragon was shivering … shivering like a dog that had been told to stay, and was staying, even when a delicious ham bone sat before it.

"You're hungry, I know," she said, bringing the goat to it. "So hungry! Here's some tasty goat for you. Maybe we can give you another one when you get done with this one."

Now the dragon looked at her – its golden eyes zeroed in on her … saw her.

The first time its eyes had zeroed in on hers, she'd felt like a mouse under the eye of a hawk.

This time … this time, her heart shivered. It shivered in the same way the dragon was shivering.

It was something she'd longed for so desperately, now that Neva had been driven away, now that her grandpapa was gone, now that Teita was all shut up from grief.

A friend.

The size of her longing caught her by surprise. "I hope we can be friends," she said softly. "Please. You've lost everything too, and you're among strangers, and I bet you don't know what's going to become of you. Let me help you. Let's be friends. Okay?"

She lay the goat down and stepped back, trying to swallow past the big lump that had suddenly appeared in her throat.

The dragon looked at her. In one swift movement, it rose, and for a moment Fia wanted to spring backwards. But she didn't move, not wanting to startle it.

The dragon moved forward to eat the goat. But instead of eating, it lifted its head and snuffled at Fia's hands, stretching its neck out, and the super-heated air of its breath rushed over her.

She didn't dare to breathe, to move.

Slowly, the dragon lowered its head to her hands, which were now shaking slightly. It touched its forehead to her fingertips. Its eyes closed.

Fia could scarcely believe her eyes.

"Oh, dragon," she breathed. Intense joy welled up in her heart like cool spring waters. Gently, she laid her hand flat on its forehead, the horned, emerald carapace surprisingly cool compared to the heat coming off the rest of its body. The dragon's head was immense, and with its horns it was about the same size as Fia's torso. Yet it bowed its head to her and touched her hand as gently as a cat. This close to it, she could see the glitter of sparks in the gemlike emerald scales, the rainbow-like iridescence in one of its horns that caught the lantern's gleam just so.

Fia's heart beat high in her chest.

"Thank you, dragon," she whispered. "Thank you."

But now she could see its wounds, uncovered, probably fly-blown by now.

"We need to clean up your wounds," she said quietly. "You're going to get sick if we can't take care of you. Can you let us help you? Can you trust us?"

The dragon's eyes opened. With its tongue, it licked her hand, just the barest of touch. Then it turned at last to its food and began eating messily as if starving.

Fia stepped back, laughter bubbling up inside her, but she stayed serious. "Will you be able to show me how to clean these wounds?" she asked Messer Albizzi.

"Gladly," he said quietly, awe in his voice.

"And maybe we can take the manacles off the dragon's feet," she added quietly. "So we can wash it."

"Bring another goat," Messer Albizzi said quietly to his son, who was watching with what seemed to be wonder. He shook himself awake and hurried into the goat pen.

Fia felt about to burst from joy. The dragon was finishing the goat, but she was watching Fia. When their eyes met, the dragon held the gaze for a moment before she went back to eating. She happily ate the next goat that they prepared for her, then the next.

When she was full at last, she lay her head down on her feet and watched Fia with some curiosity. Now Fia was bolder and gently touched the dragon's nose with her fingertips.

The dragon flinched only slightly, but it stayed still, its golden eyes gleaming like flames, fixed only on her. Its nose was hot, its breath was hotter, but that wasn't why Fia could hardly breathe. That was because of the great sense of awe that filled her heart … her joy.

*I'm just a girl, but this war dragon **trusts** me.*

"My name is Fia," she said. "And I guess you need a name … I'll call you Ryelleth."

And someday, Fia swore, *someday, you and I can go and find Neva, and help her, wherever she is.*

But first …

"Let's get your wounds cleaned up and dressed," she said quietly. "We'll get a bucket of clean water, take those manacles off your feet, and get started. Can we do that?"

The dragon's mouth opened slightly, and Fia realized that it was smiling in the same way a dog smiled. Then it lowered its head and gently nudged her, as if in assent.

She smiled back. "Thank you, Ryelleth. Thank you for trusting me."

The emerald dragon raised her head and gazed deeply in Fia's eyes.

"Yes," Fia whispered, her heart beating high with happiness as she stroked the dragon's face. "Yes, let's be friends."

* * *

Thanks so much for reading. Be sure to take a minute to leave a review!

The full, completed DRAGONRIDERS OF FIORENZA series is available now – order the first book, Assassin's Blade, here! (Note: The first chapter in that book will be the same as the first chapter in this story, but THEN the whole rest of the series will be completely new material.)

THE DRAGONRIDERS OF FIORENZA

Why not splurge on my completed six-book series about a young dragonrider in 1200s Florence, and her fiercely loyal dragon Ryelleth. They love each other with all their hearts and they are ready to set the world on fire to keep from being separated.

Assassin's Blade
Dragon's Inferno
Guardian's Race
Witch's Plight
Warrior's Doom
Traitor's Oath

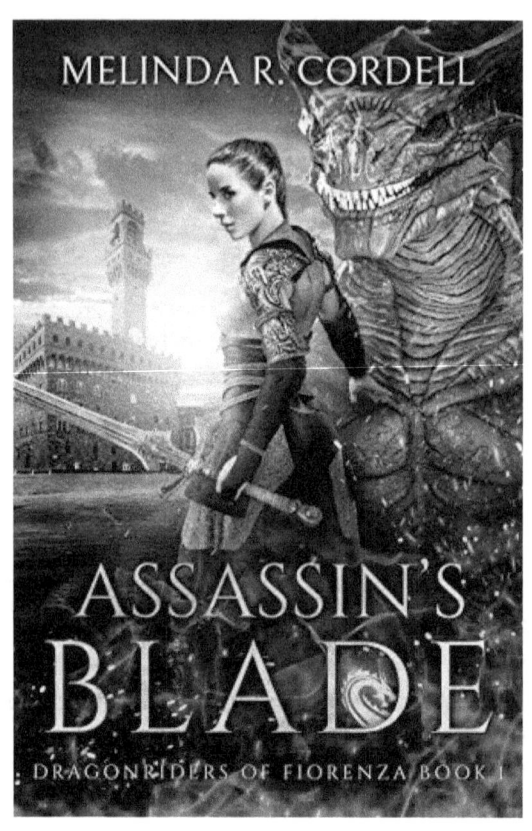

MELINDA R. CORDELL

ASSASSIN'S
BLADE

DRAGONRIDERS OF FIORENZA BOOK 1

And if you enjoyed this story, be sure to order
The Flame of Battle – the first book in the
ongoing DRAGONRIDERS OF SKALA series.
It's like Game of Thrones, only with Vikings
and more dragons and undead revenants.
And it's going to be a blast.

1 – A FINAL GOODBYE

A cold wind gusted in from the sea. Its fine spray broke over Dyrfinna's arms as she and her friends each carried a heavy-laden chest to Thora's funeral ship. They walked closely together, and the scent of her friend's room floated off the chest, soon to be devoured by fire. Dyrfinna's heart was too full of pain for her to speak.

Dyrfinna squinted against the wind, the late afternoon sun burning her eyes. Or maybe those were tears. She was not particularly interested in reviewing her emotions at the moment.

The pyre for the Queen's daughter had been raised on the shoreline for her burning journey to Helgafjell, the holy mountain, to join the kinfolk who had gone before her. The great funerary boat had been dragged onto the pebbly shore, surrounded by silent crowds of Vikings.

Once aboard, Dyrfinna set down the heavy chest for a moment and climbed up next to the prow of the ship to stand on the rail next to the dragon's head, which had been reattached to the ship for its final voyage. How many times had Dyrfinna stood balanced here in the old days with her sword, her unbound hair blowing in the breeze, doing sword exercises and enjoying the feeling of flight as the ship leapt through the waves.

The sturdy karvi ship had been Thora's favorite when she was alive, and she used to take her friends – her special guard – on excursions along the coast. Skeggi would recite poetry. Rjupa would sit next to Thora, singing along with the poem. Thora would try to ignore the book that she'd brought along – she could never go anywhere without a book – but she'd end up reading it anyway. Dyrfinna would stand balanced next to the prow doing sword exercises while Gefjun and Ostryg leaned over the sides, annoying the fishes.

But now the ship was prepared for burning, with dry peat and tarred wood filling the upper deck up to the oaken gunnels.

While they made a bed upon the kindling for Thora, the dragons stood over them, waiting to accompany Thora on her final voyage, their gemlike scales glittering like garnets and gold from their internal fires. Thora's garnet dragon, Serja, puffed hot air over Thora's body, trying to keep the flies at bay as they gathered around her face and tried to crawl into her mouth and nostrils.

"Our poor girl," the dragon said softly. Dyrfinna walked to them, balancing on the rail. Thora's dragon had long horns and thin, hairlike feathers behind the horns and around her ears. Their face was narrow, like a deer's, only with smooth scales that gleamed with their own internal fires when the wind blew on them. Dyrfinna stroked Serja's feathers as she gazed on Thora. Her thigh accidentally got too close to Serja's golden collar, and a small spark of magic popped against her leg. She moved without thinking.

"We cannot believe that Thora's gone," Serja said with a shiver through their great wings, folded neatly at their sides. "She just flicked out of life so quickly, like a mayfly."

"I know." Dyrfinna laid her head on the dragon's nose, feeling the warmth of their internal fires, and the quiet song the dragon was humming to itself.

Now that Thora was gone, Dyrfinna was going to lose the life she loved. No dragons, no glorious flights, no weapons training with the best instructors, no studies in military tactics. Now that Thora was gone, nothing would stand between her and her father's anger.

Dyrfinna was a demoted dragonrider – not even a dragonrider any more, after today.

She breathed deeply. *This is not about me,* she thought. *Put that out of your mind. Today our nation is in mourning. I can weep and bemoan my fate tomorrow.*

"Come, Dyrfinna," Rjupa said in a sad voice, and Dyrfinna kissed the dragon's nose and hopped down, turning to face what she didn't want to see.

Thora had been laid upon the kindling, wearing her green dress of thick wool, lavishly embroidered with gold, and a wide belt of exquisitely tooled leather around her waist. Dyrfinna, along with her friends, adjusted her dress so it lay beautifully around Thora's body, set her long, golden braids over her shoulders, and lay gold coins to cover her half-open eyes. They set a delicate gold band on her forehead and adorned her neck with a necklace with beads of gold and amber.

Dyrfinna set the handle of Thora's axe into her stiff, unbending hand as best she could, lay her swords at her right side, and propped her golden shield at her left side. In the meanwhile, Gefjun set her armor out within easy reach and nestled roses and other flowers in her hair.

Rjupa, her tears falling thick, set down Thora's well-worn books that only a few in the land could read – some written in Latin, some in runes. The calfskin covers had been rubbed soft by Thora's hands.

Finally, Dyrfinna knelt at Thora's side and laid her hnefatafl game, king's table, next to her body, with the amber game pieces in a small drawskin bag. Yielding to an impulse, she opened the bag and poured the pieces into her hand to look at them one last time. The amber markers clicked in her hand – half of them a rich, dark orange, the other half of them a lighter orange. The king's piece, with its small crown, stood above the other pieces, translucent, almost glowing in the afternoon sun. Like Thora's books, this, too, had been worn smooth by constant use.

How many times had Dyrfinna and Thora bent their heads over these pieces on the hnefatafl board, mulling through different strategies to capture the king? How many long afternoons like this one had flowed past until the sun hung low in the window of the keep, and Thora's servant appeared in the doorway to say, "The Queen would like you to come to dinner one of these days. She has called you at least fifty times." Her servant had a knack for overstatement. But Thora would frown a bit, her eyes never leaving the board, and say, "Wait a moment, I'm about to capture Finna's king," and the poor servant would have to wait, hoping that the Queen wouldn't have to call her fifty more times.

Now Dyrfinna looked for a long moment at her friend's bluish face, the smell of decay filling her nostrils.

"This isn't right," she said, grieved anew, and gently poured the pieces back into their bag.

"I know," Gefjun said from behind Dyrfinna, gazing fiercely down at their friend's corpse, the sun blazing through her long red hair. "It's not right. She was too young to die." She reached out and gave Dyrfinna a hand up. Gefjun always became sharp when she was deeply upset, and often when she wasn't.

"Sometimes it happens," Rjupa said quietly, joining them, tears shimmering in her eyes. She was a small woman with delicate features, but today she wore the war-prize she had earned: The gigantic helmet of Iron Skull, pitted with the marks of many swords and axes. It dwarfed her face, but she wore it with deserved pride. "Many people die young."

"But why *did* she die?" Gefjun asked Rjupa. "She fell sick while visiting King Varinn, but everybody said it wasn't bad. She seemed fine when she came home, only tired and sneezy. Then the next day she collapsed in the garden and died."

"I don't know," Rjupa said softly. "It seems wrong. But nobody knows why the Nornir choose to cut the thread of somebody's life."

"Oh, I'll tell the Norns what I think of that," Gefjun snapped.

"Take care what you say about the deathless gods," Dyrfinna warned.

"Oh, stop, Finna. Even if they did come for me, you'd fight the Fates themselves just to be belligerent."

Dyrfinna wasn't sure if this was a complaint or a compliment, so she let it go. "Rjupa's right. But ..." She blew out a hard gust of air, gazing again at Thora. "If there had been any way that I could have died in her place, I would have. I would have much rather died in her place."

Those words had surprised Dyrfinna as soon as they came out, and she felt the full weight of them. So did her friends. Now they were both quiet, gazing at her, worried.

She instantly looked down and her heart convulsed. "I didn't mean it like that," she added, low.

Gefjun and Rjupa exchanged a glance. Then Rjupa laid a small hand on Dyrfinna's back. "There's no use in second-guessing yourself," she said gently. "This can't be easy, coming so soon after your brother's ... death."

If that what you choose to call it. "I know," Dyrfinna said, low. A huge, nameless anguish fell over her, and she turned away.

"Yeah, everybody's talking about it. I mean, how Thora died," Gefjun said roughly as Dyrfinna turned back. "Because you don't die of a *cold*. You just don't. She didn't even have a fever." Gefjun was a healer, dedicated to her work, her clothes always smelling of sage and thyme and other herbs. "It doesn't make sense."

The men of the village were bringing on board ship the other provisions that Thora would need in the next world – wine, bread, and her horse, who was led onto the ship and killed, beautifully harnessed and equipped. Her house goods were brought aboard and carefully arranged around her body. All of the jewelry and gold she owned glittered in the streaming light of the afternoon sun. Roman coins were thrown around her, along with coins from the Balkans, Andalusia, and the Berber Kingdom, all the riches of the queen's only child.

"The dwellers at Helgafjell will see how much we loved her," Rjupa said in her small, broken voice, "when she comes sailing up to their holy mountain with all these riches."

"I only wish we had more books to send with her," Dyrfinna said.

The other girls laughed, despite their tears.

Now Dyrfinna smiled. She imagined what it would be like when Thora sailed to the holy mountain. Thora would sail out of the mist of life into the next world on her ship, her riches ranged about her, her horse whickering at her back. The residents of the holy mountain, the dead of the ages before, would gather on the shore to receive the young queen and greet her – and she'd take no notice of them because she would be sitting on a bench on the boat with her feet up, reading a book.

So where did your brother end up when you killed him? Dyrfinna asked herself. *Which shore did his ship carry him to? You denied him entry into Valhalla, for he was not killed in battle or in defending himself. Would he have gone to Hel instead?*

"The tide is coming in," somebody called from the shore, breaking her out of these dark thoughts.

Taking a deep breath, Dyrfinna looked around Thora's ship. Most everything was in good order and ready for Thora's final voyage. She exhaled gustily, rubbed her eyes, and turned away.

Just because they were shield maidens didn't mean they couldn't weep.

One of the men lay a pair of open scissors on Thora's chest, and her feet were tied together to keep her from walking after death. Dyrfinna shook her head at their worries. She would be going out to sea. Her draugr would not be able to walk back from a sea-burial.

The young women climbed back down from the funeral pyre and hopped off the side of the ship. The tide was well in by now, and they splashed into ankle-deep water to walk to dry sand, the waves swooshing around their legs. It touched the bottom of Thora's boat, but not enough yet to lift it. But this would quickly change, as her shallow-drafted boat could sail in low water that would ground most any other boat.

The sun was setting in glory, reds and oranges suffusing the sky across the great expanse of salt water. The great mountains of the fjords stood in silent grandeur under the changing sky.

Dyrfinna glanced over her shoulder. There, faces ruddy in the light of the sunset and the faint glow of the garnet dragons, came the rest of her sword-friends – Ostryg and Skeggi. Ostryg put his big arm around Gefjun's shoulders, while Rjupa leaned against Skeggi for support. They were couples. Dyrfinna was the odd one out.

The sword-friends were also Thora's guard, raised to defend her in all things. They wore matching cloaks that were clasped with a silver brooch that represented Corae, the dragon who had died defending them and Thora.

In the crowd were the kings and jarls that ruled the kingdoms and principalities that ranged across the land, a patchwork of rivalries and factions.

Looking across the crowd, she saw a face she hadn't seen before among the kings and jarls that stood by the sea – a group of Moors, and standing in their midst was a great man who was completely undone, his face a mask of tears as he gazed at Thora's ship.

"Who's that fellow? Is he one of the kings?" she asked, noting the ermine fur that edged his cloak, the subtle golden band on his head.

Skeggi nodded. "That's not just any king. That's King Varinn himself. If Thora hadn't died, he would have been our king as well, once the Queen died."

"Maybe," Dyrfinna said, since only the Nornir knew what was to come. Varinn's people had come from either Toledo or Castille, she hadn't been quite clear on which, before her grandparents' time.

"She would have been the best of queens," Rjupa said sadly in her small voice. "He's lost a treasure. We all have."

Dyrfinna nodded, her jaw tightening. She was to lead them in the sky dance of the dragons.

This is going to be the last time I can ride a dragon, she thought, and nearly felt the tears come on.

She cleared her throat, pushed her grief away. This was not the time. "Are you ready?"

Gefjun leaned on Dyrfinna. Her hair was twisted up in a loose bun, though many red tendrils had escaped. She wore her old burgundy tunic, as usual – nothing fancy because she spent a lot of time gathering herbs with her mother, or digging in the garden, or practicing swords. She was a beautiful young woman, but careless of her beauty.

"No," she said roughly. "I am not ready for this. I hate the world and everything in it, that Thora had to die."

Ostryg clapped a hand on Gefjun's shoulder. "Death comes for us all," he said.

Dyrfinna growled, "What a thing to say at a funeral."

His eyes snapped to hers. "That's because it's the truth," he said. "You smelled her up there. There's no way to pretty that up. Besides," he said, his voice softening as he turned a tender look down on Gefjun, "We have work to do. We can give in to our grief later."

Rjupa's face was a mask of tears under Iron Skull's helmet. Thora had been kindest to her when she was a thrall who had escaped from and killed the cruel warrior, so Thora's death had hit her especially hard. "I hope you don't hold it against me if I give in to my grief now," she said quietly.

Dyrfinna's heart was low. "I don't. Not at all. Thora's last moments with us are drawing to a close."

READ MORE in THE FLAME OF BATTLE, now available at your favorite book retailers.

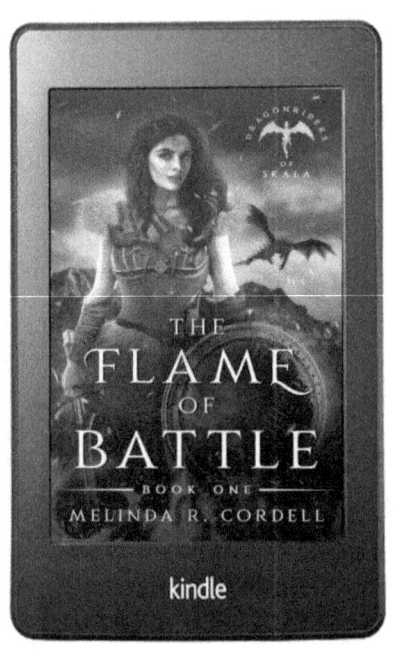

*This was me back in 1995 at the beginning of my writing
career.
I was a real writing hotshot back then.
To tell the truth, I still am.*

About the Author

Melinda R. Cordell has written a truckload of
YA novels, including the Dragonriders of
Skala series (like *Game of Thrones*, with Vikings),
and her newest series, the Dragonriders of
Fiorenza, currently in progress.

A former city horticulturist and a long-time
garden writer, Melinda has also written 12 books
in the Easy-Growing Gardening series and now is

starting the Hungry Garden series under the name Rosefiend Cordell.

Melinda lives in northwest Missouri with her husband and two kids, the best little family to walk the earth, and is writing about 24 books at once, fueled by passion and caffeine.

If you want to keep up with her, subscribe to her newsletter, to get a YA dragon adventure called *A Whisper of Smoke*, set in Viking times. Or drop her a friendly note at rosefiend@gmail.com. She'll reply! If she doesn't reply, she didn't get your email, or she completely flaked, so try again.

Follow her on Patreon to get a behind-the-scenes look at this author's world. See new book covers, read excerpts of upcoming stories before anybody else does, help her name characters, and superfans get to show up on her novels!

Don't forget to leave a book review on your favorite retailer, as well as BookBub, or Goodreads.

Join Melinda Online
Melindacordell.com
BookBub
Facebook
Twitter

The Dragonriders of Fiorenza series

www.ingramcontent.com/pod-product-compliance
Lightning Source LLC
Chambersburg PA
CBHW051514260626
47162CB00008B/2972